ISBN 1-4116-5483-8

The Parable of Miriam the Camel Driver

written by Murphy

TABLE OF CONTENTS

Part the First 2
Part the Second 4
Part the Third 7
Part the Fourth 10
Part the Fifth 13
Part the Sixth 16
Part the Seventh 19
Part the Eighth 22
Part the Ninth 25
Part the Tenth 29
Part the Eleventh 32
Part the Twelfth 35
Part the Thirteenth 38
Part the Fourteenth 41
Part the Fifteenth 44
Part the Sixteenth 47
Part the Seventeenth 50
Part the Eighteenth 53

Part the Nineteenth..........56
Part the Twentieth..........59
Part the Twenty First..........62
Part the Twenty Second..........65
Part the Twenty Third..........68
Part the Twenty Fourth..........71
Part the Twenty Fifth..........75
Part the Twenty Sixth..........78
Part the Twenty Seventh..........81
Part the Twenty Eighth..........84
Part the Twenty Ninth..........87
Part the Thirtieth..........90
Part the Thirty First..........93
Part the Thirty Second..........96
Part the Thirty Third..........100
Part the Thirty Fourth..........103
Part the Thirty Fifth..........106
Part the Thirty Sixth..........109
Part the Thirty Seventh..........112
Part the Thirty Eighth..........115

Thanks to Chris for all his encouragement. And thanks to Wendee, Lynda, Telissa, the ladies of Larchmont, and of course my mother.

Part the First

Long ago but not so far away the young woman Miriam found her way to the big city. She came with her very small bag and her beloved lute to see what she could find.

Miriam was fascinated by the bustle of the city. With big eyes she watched all the people go by from a seat alone in the corner. Everyone passed through her gaze—so many people of every kind. The people of power came and went: royalty; the moneymen; those with things to sell and buy; architects building monuments for antiquity, for a price, or both; the sophists; the artists.

She watched them move quick and quiet over the city. They could be fast and ferocious, dealing with one another. Miriam imagined they had maps behind their eyes. They knew exactly where they were headed and what they wanted.

Miriam walked among the fast paced and did not feel the current. Everyone else was pushed or pulling. She remained unmoved, a dry rock jutting above the rushing river.

In abandoned sentry corners, Miriam sat with her lute as her only companion. Tracing winding melodies, her fingers found paths not traveled. She pondered the lives passing in front of her eyes. Miriam imagined she was invisible; no one could see her. Certainly no one looked at her. What did other people need her for? She was small and unimportant in a very significant place. She thought about what it must be like to be large—casting a shadow of power and substance.

Miriam weighed her own value as she sat in the corner and came up wanting. In this busy world, thinking thoughts and playing songs were not enough. It was time to dive into the river.

"That's exactly what I need to do," Miriam thought. "But I have no idea where to begin. How do I launch myself?"

Part the Second

Miriam began to struggle for an admission past the impenetrable facade of other people's importance. The people walking past had attained a new significance. They had the right of way. These others knew the secret password to get in. They had lives of relevance, and any of them—all she needed was just one of them—could let her in.

But how? Why should any of these busy people help her? "I have nothing to offer anyone in return," Miriam thought. "Why should anyone even notice me?"

And they didn't. They didn't pay any attention to her at all. She was less than the ground they tread. She thought she could start by trying merely to be seen. Scared and nervous, she gathered up her courage to get someone's attention. That would be a big start.

"If I could just ask a few questions, I'd be able to learn how to find a way…I'd just ask some questions."

But the river of humanity rushed, and no one wanted to take time for Miriam. The men of power only looked to their own path, not glancing to the left or right. The buyers and sellers argued with one another unceasingly. The money and the monuments were hard to interrupt.

She had little hope as she leaned against the city gate. She had met no friendly glance since she had begun her mission. More people were here at the entrance than almost anywhere else, but they had no time to spare. A herd of camels stopped in front of her, waiting patiently to move on to their stables.

Miriam reached up to scratch the neck of the camel nearest her. He leaned into the pleasure of the scratch and attention.

Miriam smiled at him, “At least you appreciate me,” she murmured.

“He likes you,” a voice behind her spoke.

Startled, she turned to see a short man in a dusty blue cloak. “Sorry to surprise you. I’m the one in charge of these beasts. They call me Micah the camel driver.”

Part the Third

"You want to know about camels?" Micah said.

"Can you teach me?" Miriam asked.

"I've been knowing camels for a long, long time. I can tell you more than you want to know." He reached up and began to untie the bundle on his camel's back. "Lend a hand; that's the best way to learn."

He showed her how to unload the pack so it came down easily. There was a specific way to do all the little things these camel journeys required. The order mattered very much. "You can make it easy on yourself, or you can do it the hard way. Pay attention, and you'll see."

He let her help him, giving her a chance to go along on the camel journeys. The routes, the oases, the food and water and all the comforts that the important people taking the journey needed—

Micah showed her what it took to be a successful camel driver.

He was very successful. He had his own camels and was in high demand from royal and powerful people. He could pick and choose the journeys he would take. He chose Miriam to come along and meet all the other people along the way—the camel dealers, the people who provided and prepared the supplies. It took a lot of help to get all the pieces in place.

This was a rich city and many, many people had to travel for all kinds of reasons. Micah showed her how to talk with the patrons to get the best pay and to be sure that the details of the journey were clear.

After what seemed to Miriam a very long time, she was able to lead her own camel drives. Micah did not want her to go, but Miriam was anxious to go on her own.

“You’ve learned a lot, Miriam. There is certainly enough work for you to go on your own. Good luck!” Micah would miss her, she could tell. She owed him a lot.

She was very busy with work and learning a lot more about how to make it on her own. Being the solely responsible person on these camel drives was harder than she had believed. But she found out her own possibilities and did a good job.

“I’m very good at this,” she thought. “I really am in the thick of things now.” It was exciting, but after long days of work Miriam missed making music with her lute.

“I should find a way to make time for what really matters. As exciting as the drives are, my lute is much more important to me than camels.”

Part the Fourth

The demand for camel drives did not slow down—it seemed to increase. Miriam did her best to find time to play. She brought the lute along and entertained the camels after their day's work. She wanted to become a truly excellent musician and made some progress on her own.

She made friends now on her journeys and in the city. Some of them were from her work, and some were fellow musicians and artists. Miriam liked best the friends who shared both interests.

The camel drives took most of her attention. All the important people with their journeys needed her, and it felt pretty good to get the job done. The rush and bustle were exactly what the big city life was about, and she was part of that life.

But the swell of business crested and broke. Gradually—then quickly—the demand for journeys dried up. Fewer requests for her services came.

There came a time when she had to look hard to find people who needed a camel driver.

Everyone in the city was having a hard time. People were calling it a famine. For miles around, things were slowing. The people stopped coming and going. Miriam realized that it would be some time before her camel commerce could be restored.

There remained a few frantic crossings to keep her busy, but Miriam knew things would come to a halt—and soon. People did not need to make journeys because there was no longer any trade. The royalty shook their heads and put their hands in their empty pockets. "What will I do?" she thought. Everyone in the city and all around seemed trapped in fear about how to survive this calamity.

Miriam counted her possessions. "I have been careful," she realized with relief. "I knew how to be frugal before I became a camel driver, and I have not forgotten. If I am careful, I can go without work for quite some time."

The prospect of a large empty space of time stood before her. Suddenly, it seemed a gift. "I will apprentice myself to a lute Master. I have always dreamed of such a thing, but I never thought I would have the opportunity. Now, with the gold I've earned with my camels, I can make my wish come true."

Miriam sold the extra camels and all the other things she would not need. She said goodbye to her friends in the city and set off with her one camel to an apprenticeship for the lute.

She was sad to leave her dear friends and the busy city she loved, but the joy of making and listening to beautiful music lay before her.

Part the Fifth

Miriam had to travel some distance to reach the guildhall that would take her on as apprentice. It was a respectable guild—and not small.

The hall was filled with students of music. Many lute players were there and even more students of other instruments. The place was bathed in music. It was all anyone spoke or thought about. There were exercises to memorize and ancient Masters to study.

Some of the work was easy and fun. Some of it stretched her abilities brutally and took her further than she'd ever been before. Other times the Master teachers required her to do things that made no sense whatsoever. Miriam could not argue. They were the Masters. They were her teachers. And if she wanted to achieve Master status she had to do as they asked.

The apprentice guild was very different than life in the big city. The city had all kinds of people flowing through. Here at the guildhall, everyone had a single interest. If the city had been a river, the guild was a vortex circling around the same spot again and again.

But there was momentum here, too. Miriam loved to be able to talk and play music with so many other experienced and quality artists. These Master teachers and students worked on understanding music from long ago. It was exciting and endlessly fascinating to get into closer and finer inspection of how the old Masters had practiced their craft.

Miriam admired the old Masters very much, but she found the guild's attitude difficult to understand. "Why are we studying how other people made music? I can make my own music, but no one here is interested."

Truly, Miriam did not have much time to make her own music. The effort required to achieve new levels and pass through her apprenticeship swallowed her time and energy. Miriam worked to distinguish herself and had some success. Her teachers praised her, and she felt proud.

"I wish I could become a true Master lute player—to be like the great ones we study." The teachers made it clear: to become a great Master required even higher levels of studious achievement. It was exciting to think that she could study and pass on to become a great Master.

She was so happy! She had dreamed her whole life of being a Master of the lute. And now she was about to achieve it.

Part the Sixth

Miriam stood with her fellow apprentices in a straight line, each one formally holding their own instrument. It was a formal ceremony, but the musicians' hands grasped their tool with practiced experience. By this time, the instruments had become extensions of their own bodies.

They had all studied and engaged in the trials and assessments. Each one had been examined for strengths and weaknesses. Their diligence and patience were tried. All those standing were about to have the honor of Master musician conveyed upon them.

The Master teachers gave each one their recognition, and Miriam could hardly believe she had made it. All her fellow musicians, all the work they had done and the knowledge they had gained in this place—it couldn't be over.

The Master teachers had encouraged her greatly. They loved the lute as much as she did and perhaps even more. She had been encouraged to stay, to learn more and to attain higher levels. It seemed so tempting to stay in this oasis of music and mastery.

For many days and weeks after the ceremony, Miriam planned to continue on with her study of the lute. She thought about how to stay on, and she began to plan for it.

Certain details began to bother her. The Master teachers required money for their services. And Miriam and her camel needed to eat and otherwise take care of themselves. How would she find means to pay for this while she was studying? And there was one other nagging problem.

"I came to the city to get into the current of things. This guildhall feels completely outside of the rest of the world. It thrills me to be with music lovers. But at the same time, they only love a certain type of music. There seems to be no place for my music and my own lute playing. I can only play they way they want. I have to find my own way."

The practical realities Miriam had learned to respect as a camel driver—the need for food, shelter and a good direction—were the louder voice in her decision.

"It's fine to be a lute master, but I must take care of myself." Miriam packed her small bag and loaded her camel. She counted the few coins in her purse and set off to see who might need to ride some camels over the horizon.

Part the Seventh

Where did they need the services of a camel driver? Miriam's first thought was to return to the city she had left. But the famine continued, and her city had been the worst hit. As she heard from her friends—saw the hunger in their eyes and the fear in their voices—she began to feel anxious.

It was obvious she would need to look elsewhere to find a way to feed herself. She journeyed to the busy oases, the places where all the camels and drivers had to stop to rest. She had often been approached at these places; people had wanted her services for their camel drives.

Now it was eerily quiet. There were camels, to be sure, but much fewer than before. And there were shiftless camel drivers asking everyone for the exact thing Miriam had come for: work.

This was bad. Miriam had an excellent reputation, but what good did that do when everyone was equally unknown? She left that oasis.

"I'm going to have to go further to find what I'm looking for," Miriam realized. She directed her camel to the next city.

She was beginning to be afraid. So many people were struggling. She worried that she would run to the end of her resources and still have no help. With this thought she lashed her camel to go faster.

The beast barked his complaint at this treatment. Miriam had to stop to reassure him and gain his good graces again. She laughed at herself—an attempt to bolster her courage.

"I have to believe that I will find what I need. The world is wide, and I will keep looking. There is every chance I will find a place in this new city." Miriam smiled. "And this place is famous for its excellent lute players. I'll at least be able to meet with other lute masters. There is always that to look forward to."

But her heart beat fast and heavy, thinking of what might be in store.

Part the Eighth

"We are looking to keep camels. The royal family has decided more camel drives are necessary. You would certainly seem to be what we are looking for, Miriam."

At last! This man, an overseer for the royalty of the city, was offering her work as the royal camel driver. This could be the chance she feared would never come. Here in this new city she would be safe and have enough of what she needed.

The man kept talking: "You would be given a tent within reach of the camels, and of course the royals whom you serve would give you various rewards for your service. They are known for being generous to their slaves."

Miriam jerked her head back. "The royal camel driver is a slave?"

The overseer's weathered face stretched into a smile. "Of course. It is our culture. That is how we have always done things. It works out best that way. After you have been here some time you will see. We are all a family and look out for one another. Believe me, it is a good system."

Miriam needed to think about what this would mean. She asked and was given a day to decide.

"What's to decide?" she thought. "I need to have a way to take care of myself." She thought about her options. When she had learned to drive camels, she had done it in perfect freedom. It hadn't been necessary to sign up for slavery. "But maybe the overseer is right. This is the way things are done. It has been this way for a long time."

How could she fight city tradition? They had been doing it this way for a long time. It probably was for the best. The royal family arranged matters this way because it worked well for everyone. The man said they looked out for each other.

Miriam thought about it all day. "The important thing for me is to be able to make my music. I can't do that if I don't have a way to live."

She slept that night, and by the morning she had decided. This would be her new home. She would start her life as the royal camel driver—a slave.

Part the Ninth

"There you go, boy. It will have to do for now." Miriam patted her camel as he ate from his trough. "I'll make it nicer here before long. I promise." His stable needed a lot of work before it was ready for him. The other camels looked unhappy. The whole place needed work.

"At least my quarters are acceptable." They were as nice as anything she had ever had. Miriam felt reassured that, despite her slave status, things were going to work out.

With hope for her new city, Miriam began to organize the camels. The days passed as she brushed them out and bound their broken hooves. She knew how to care for them, and they began to look handsome. It made Miriam proud.

But that was only the start, and she knew it. A camel driver must understand the routes. What outposts and oases did they use? What workers and resources were available? The success of the journey was dependent on the comfort of the royals. What special luxuries would they need?

For having such a pack of raggedy camels, these royals were very persnickety. It was immediately obvious that in order to make them happy she would need help from the other slaves.

Her group—the slaves under the same overseer—refused to help her. What else could she do? Looking around, Miriam saw a different set of slaves well-situated to help her. Their overseer, a woman with a reputation for common sense, had a large group of slaves at her command. But as soon as Miriam approached those slaves for help, they found reasons to be elsewhere.

Their belligerence aggravated Miriam. Didn't they care about their work? Didn't they have pride in doing a job well?

After she had asked and asked, one man finally told her. "Miriam, we are slaves. It's a bad idea to volunteer for anything. Just take care of the camels and leave the rest alone. We can't help you."

Miriam didn't understand how the slaves could act that way, and she wanted no part of their behavior. Strumming her lute at home, she rebelled against the slave attitude. "I am proud of my camels, and I know we can make the royals comfortable during their drives. I will find a way. I know what to do, and I am good at doing it."

She still needed some help. She decided to go to her overseer. She wanted him to make the request to the other overseer. If their own overseer ordered those slaves to assist, they would have to. Wouldn't they?

Her overseer allowed Miriam an audience. She bowed low, looked at him and said, "Sir, the camels are ready for their journey. But there are many necessities still to prepare. I need help from the other slaves to complete the preparations."

The overseer looked back at her. “Silence, slave. By what authority do you speak to me? Your job is to care for the camels. Who asked you to prepare for the journey? Leave me and do not return.”

Part the Tenth

Miriam wept as she brushed her camels. There was no help from her overseer. How could he speak to her that way? This must be what it meant to be a slave. He was not a slave. Not all the people she worked with were slaves.

But Miriam was. And she was on her own with no help to prepare for her journeys. She brushed at her tears and thought, "Maybe that slave was right. Maybe I should not do any more than necessary. But it seems stupid to have good camels and not prepare for the rest of the journey. When the saddles are hard, or there is not enough water, or the outposts don't expect us and have no food, the journey will be miserable. How are those things not necessary? It takes much more than healthy camels to make a camel drive."

The people at the outposts understood. She sent messages to them to make such preparations as they could. They were very happy to help—glad that she was giving them time to get ready and letting them know what the royal family expected. At least Miriam could do that much.

Her lute was a great comfort at that time. She found circles of other lute layers and played with them. “It doesn’t matter if I am a slave,” she thought. “I am a lute master, and that’s the most important thing to me.” She brought it to these new camels and played for them.

Why couldn’t the overseer see the need for the preparations as she did? It was ridiculous to set out on a camel drive only half prepared. She went to the other slaves again, trying to find a way.

Miriam discovered that while the other slaves wouldn’t help her, they had no objection to her using their tools and supplies to do the work in their stead. “This is so ridiculous,” she thought. “Even slaves ought to be better than this.” But she wanted to be able to do the job right. After all, she was part of the caravan as well as the royals. Things began to go much more smoothly.

But the overseer was not pleased. “Slave! I told you: camels are your job. Stick to your own work!”

Miriam kept her eyes down at this rebuke. She said nothing. Now she understood that she would have to be as quiet as possible. She could not draw attention to herself as she got ready for her journeys.

Many of the camel and saddle merchants told her, “Your camels are so beautiful now! We remember how rough they looked before. And your tack is so well cared for. This royal family must be so glad to have you here in charge.”

Of course Miriam smiled at that. Yes, the royals who drove with her were happy. But she was not in charge—far from it.

Part the Eleventh

The overseer was cruel to everyone. He despised Miriam, but his favorites suffered even more. He watched them as they worked—telling them to do it his way even when it was wrong. He treated them as his friends, and they only wanted to get away.

Miriam thought, "If only I could get away from this overseer I could get help. He makes me so miserable." She was very busy, tending the camels and also making all the preparations for the journeys. She began to neglect her lute.

"I am still a lute master," she said. "I will find a way to get the help I need, and then I can pay attention to my lute. There must be a way."

As she led the journeys for the royals, they began to realize and appreciate her carefulness. She thought about asking them for help, but it was so tricky. Even if they did listen, most likely they would only tell the overseer to take care of the problems. And if the overseer heard she had talked with royalty, she would be so punished and persecuted life would barely be worth living.

She bedded her camels down at the outpost and played a sad song.

"That's beautiful."

Miriam was startled. Someone was listening? Yes, it was one of the many lesser members of the royal family who had noticed her. He asked her questions about what she did. It turned out he had responsibilities over her.

"I would like to hear more about your camel drives," he told her as he left.

"Come by again tomorrow," she said.

She did not know if she could trust him yet, but maybe he could help her. This could be her opportunity! He was the first one she had met who took her tasks seriously. She knew what she would ask him: to change to the other overseer.

When he returned, she carefully told him about what was needed. She could not tell him openly of the cruelty the overseer showed to his slaves. She was afraid he might not use discretion with such a confession. But she could tell he understood at least some of what she did not say. She only talked of how sensible it was for her to be with the other overseer, how the preparations could be made by those slaves so she would have more time to lead the caravans.

“I understand what you are saying, and I appreciate what you do,” he said. “I will help you. You must be patient, but I will get you what you need.”

Part the Twelfth

Now that Miriam had shown the journeys could be quick and comfortable, the royals wanted more and more camel drives. The King himself, who had originally despised everything about the camels, was beginning to personally order more drives for himself.

Miriam was very proud of her camels and her careful preparations. It made her happy to know that so many new journeys were happening. But it was a lot more work, with no more help. She had to be stealthy so she did not attract the attention of the overseer.

More camels had been ordered. The overseer bought them; he thought Miriam was not important enough for such tasks. The camel dealers swindled him, and the camels were wild. It took Miriam a lot of time to tame them and make them behave well enough to be driven.

Miriam had been a slave for more than a year now. With all the new work she did not have time to play her lute for the camels anymore. There were so many more drives than before. She could not lead all of them. She had to let slaves from the outposts drive them. The slaves in the city were as reluctant as ever to help.

Of course the other slaves did not really know how to drive camels. Miriam had to explain everything to them, preparing for their journeys as well as her own.

“We are buying more camels, too,” one outpost headman said. “Miriam, you understand camels better than anyone. Can’t you please choose them for us?”

Miriam cast her eyes down. “You will have to ask the overseer.” The headman took Miriam to speak to the overseer right away. She prostrated herself before him as the headman made his request.

"NO!" thundered the overseer. "She is my slave, and I do not wish it. I will purchase the camels."

So the overseer bargained with the camel dealers once more and purchased diseased camels. Miriam had to nurse them to health in between her drives. She had not touched her lute in weeks now.

But her camels were almost completely ready. She had finished brushing the last one when suddenly her legs collapsed under her. She felt the world spinning faster and faster with no way to stop it.

She closed her eyes and grabbed onto the ground. She pulled strength up from the earth and forced her voice to shout as loud as she could: "HELP ME!"

As her voice launched into the night air her world went black, and she knew no more.

Part the Thirteenth

Miriam woke up dizzy and weak. She tried to turn her head to see where she was, but she could not keep her eyes open.

"Don't try to move. You are still very sick."

She blinked and recognized the face of the healer. She must be in the healing tent. What had happened? How did she get here?

"A nearby slave heard your cry for help. We brought you here. You've been sleeping for hours."

"Hours?" she thought. "Who was taking care of the camel drives?" It didn't matter. Miriam couldn't move.

But while she had lain incapacitated, the other slaves began helping her. Now that she really needed help, they stepped in. She was so grateful to be able to rest while they did the work. Miriam was glad they had finally begun to care about the journeys and about getting them done right.

As soon as she could walk again, she went to thank them.

"We didn't know you had royal friends," they replied. "We were ordered to help you."

At last, her friend had come to help her. He had told her to be patient. But where was he? How had he known of her illness?

A message came to her: "Be careful with yourself. You need to get stronger. I ask you again to be patient. You know I have not forgotten you; I am working to take you away from the overseer."

Hope flared hot in Miriam's heart. She had a way out! She would be free from this overseer and able to pay attention to her work. Oh, it would be such a liberation not to have to sneak around to do her job well.

But he was right to tell her she needed strength. It would be a relief when she could stand up strong. Walking slowly, she found her camels and leaned on one. How long had she been a slave here in this city? Her spirit dipped low. It seemed like forever.

She was getting help now however. The other slaves were at last recognizing their duty and coming forward to make the journeys successful. And her friend remembered her.

Miriam gave a watery smile to her camel. Things would work out. They had to.

Part the Fourteenth

Walking across the courtyard, Miriam sang out loud. Her muscles rejoiced with the return of her strength. How glorious to stride with purpose and speed! Things would have to be better.

Things were coming together. The other slaves were starting to do their part; they were listening to her instructions. They were almost to the point of doing the preparations without her help.

The royals had done fewer drives during Miriam's recovery. They had not mentioned anything about it, but she appreciated their consideration. Now, however, a big journey was planned. They would stop at several outposts and Miriam had been asked to inspect the new camels at the furthest one. There was so much to do!

After checking and double-checking the camels and the bags, and after sending messages to the outposts to make sure the supplies were ready, the journey began. The camels rose together, with their riders arranged in comfort on their humps. They stretched their legs over the sand eating the distance with power and grace.

At the oasis, Miriam bedded the camels. Taking off their burdens, she smoothed and brushed their coats to keep them from galling under the saddles. They had a long way to go yet. She lay down and slept.

"By order of the Prince, why are these camels unloaded?"

Miriam blinked awake. She had been dreaming of her lute—where was she now? It was the Prince's vizier who woke her. The sun had not yet cleared the horizon.

"My Lord?" she answered.

"Our king and royal family cannot be kept waiting. The Prince passed here and saw the camels unready. They should be kept vigilant, ready to serve."

"But, Sir…" she began.

"I don't want excuses. We require you to serve with excellence! If you cannot serve, slave, we can be rid of you." His face was purple with rage. "The Prince will speak to you after you've re-loaded the camels. This must not happen again." The vizier stomped away.

Miriam looked after him, stunned. Her camels lay around her blinking peacefully. Her heart filled with pity for them. They could not stay loaded all night! What could he be asking for?

She dreaded meeting with the Prince.

Part the Fifteenth

The full circle of the dawn star shone blinding in the east when Miriam finished loading the camels for the day's journey. The Prince had ordered her to keep the camels ready at all times during the drive. But that was impossible! The beasts could not go without rest. They needed care as well as the royals.

"Miriam."

That voice—Miriam looked up. It was her friend! Her royal rescuer had come at last!

"It's been a long time since I have seen you. Have you written any new songs for your lute?" he smiled.

She gasped. Shame flooded her cheeks. Her lute was at home under a thick blanket of dust.

"I am here to escort you to see the Prince," her friend continued. "I heard about his demands.

Of course they are ridiculous. Let's wait and see, Miriam. I have hope that this will work out to our advantage."

Her courage grew from her friend. Having someone take up the burden alongside her made Miriam's legs wobbly. How long she had been carrying this alone? Too long.

The sumptuous tent of the Prince was equipped with a raised dais of rugs and pillows. He looked down from his height as they bowed to him.

"Slave, it is your work to serve us. We are the royal family, and the service of our needs cannot be delayed."

Miriam had learned enough to keep her head down. She did not need her voice—no response would be entertained.

"My Lord, our greatest pleasure is to serve the royal family."

Her friend had answered? This was very dangerous. What was he doing?

"Miriam and her camels have come under my responsibility. It has been brought to my attention that the comfort of the King and yourself, O Prince, would be better served with Miriam joining the slaves of another overseer. It is our greatest pleasure to serve you with excellence."

The Prince raised his eyebrows. "Excellent service from slaves? Let us not ask for miracles." He waved his hand, "Nevertheless, let it be as you request. You may leave us."

Part the Sixteenth

At last! Miriam did not have to worry about her overseer. She would be able to get her work done without sneaking around; she could do a good job out in the open. When the outposts asked for her help with camels, she could give it. She could buy quality camels to carry everyone the long distances right away.

Miriam's face split in two with her grin. But her friend cautioned her: "I was glad to be able to take this chance to put you where you needed to be."

"Oh, thank you! Thank you so much!" Miriam said.

He smiled back at her. "Of course. It was the right choice, the right place for you to be. But you need to realize the overseer you'll be working under now does not report to me. I won't be able to help you anymore after this."

But what help would she need now? That horrible overseer was out of her way. Now that all the slaves whose help she required had the same overseer as she did, things would flow smoothly. Her royal friend was right; it was the right place to be.

Gladness led the journey now. True, she had been forced to rise before dawn to fulfill the Prince's demands. That was how she could load the camels so they would seem always ready. But at every outpost and oasis, she told the slaves that she could help them now. Those faithful workers were so happy they all rejoiced together and gave Miriam gifts.

"We've been waiting for you to be able to help us! You are the one who understands what the camels need and what the royals want for their travels. Since you've been here, there have been so many more journeys, and we need your help. We trust you; tell us whatever needs to be done, and we will do it."

Driving the camels home at last, Miriam's heart was full. How good it was to be able to do her job well! To respect the camels and respect the other people who worked alongside her was to see respect shine from their eyes back to her. It was good to work with pride in the job well done. At the end of the long hard day of work, she could have peace in her heart.

She slept deeply in her home that night. She awoke refreshed and with a purpose. She wanted to meet with her new overseer. There was much work to be done, and they had best understand one another. But as she approached the work area of her new overseer, it seemed abandoned. What had happened?

One of the other slaves walked up to her. "Didn't you know? The overseer is gone. She found something better, I guess."

Part the Seventeenth

It was a great relief to Miriam to be free of her old overseer. But the plan to work for a different overseer was not yet finished. The overseer she had known, whom Miriam respected and looked forward to working with, had left. Who was going to take her place? What did this change mean? These questions rolled around in Miriam's head never far away from her thoughts.

Her head was overflowing with plans. On her last journey, she had promised the slaves at the outposts who had needed her help for so long that she could at last give it to them. Messages were flying in from all directions with requests, and she needed to answer them. New camel dealers came every week—nearly every day.

It was so exciting Miriam felt like she was flying. How long had she wished she could bring solutions to the problems—big and small—that she encountered during the camel drives and during the preparations. She had seen the right way to do it, seen it as clear as a bright star in the black desert sky. It was her overseer who had blocked her from reaching for it and forced her into half-measures.

Finally Miriam had her head. She could reach for the glittering star and do things the right way—the way things were meant to be done.

But more and more camel drives were being ordered. If she had not been so ecstatic, Miriam would have been terrified at how much there was to be done. As it was, she took a deep breath and told herself it would work out. The slaves she had been working with would help her. After all, they were in the same group even if they didn't have an overseer at the moment. They had begun to help her when she was sick, and now she needed their help even more.

Pushing aside the curtain entrance, she stepped into the pavilion of her new work group. Miriam was looking for the head slave and found her sorting carpets at the side. Miriam strode up to her: "I'm so glad to find you. There are several journeys for which the camels need to be ready. You'll need to make sure they are taken care of."

The head slave glared at Miriam, "Look!" she answered. "We need to get a few things straight around here. You have your work, and I have mine. Do you think I am sitting around here waiting for you to tell me what to do? I have royals waiting for their furnishings. If you need my help, just ask for it. But I am telling you, I have things to do."

"Wasn't I just asking for help?" Miriam thought. She replied carefully to the head slave. "I understand you have royals waiting for their carpets, but the camel drives are composed of royals, too. And they cannot wait at all while they are on their journey."

"You think the king's favorite cousin is going to wait for her candlestick? Or carpet? Like I said, you have your work, and I have mine. Let me know if you need help, but I've got to get back to work right now."

Part the Eighteenth

It was hard to believe. After all that had happened, Miriam was getting the cold shoulder from her new group. That head slave had helped her when she had been ill. She seemed to genuinely understand the need to do things right, even if she was a little slow on keeping the details straight.

Before Miriam had felt like this head slave was sympathetic—almost a friend. Now, she had become as cold as ice. A dull ache began in Miriam's middle. "It's not like I needed her to be a friend to get the work done," she thought. "But I had thought…as it turns out, now I have neither a friend nor help with the work."

The dull ache spread and turned from hurt to anger. "What is wrong with these people, anyway?" Miriam was jerking the saddles from their racks. "What the devil do they think they are doing? Do they sit around at the tavern and regale one another with stories of all the chores they do not do?"

She pulled out the grooming tackle to brush the camels. She began to roughly pull through the camel's fur. "They must have an empty vacuum for a soul, to take pride in doing nothing. Spare me from such small dreams!"

The camel was patient with her rough treatment. He was a fine creature. She had tamed him, and he had become a fulfilled promise. Strength and endurance were his soul's pride. "Good boy!" Miriam told him. "You just needed some help to get you on the right track. Maybe once the new overseer arrives these petty slaves will come into line again. I can imagine that a firm and consistent hand would do wonders."

Overseers did make a big difference in both directions. Her old group of slaves had been shocked and amazed when they saw that Miriam had made a clean break away. They begged to know how she'd done it. When they heard how sympathetic her royal friend was, they went to him in a group and told him all their stories. After all of them had come to him, he'd made sure that overseer wasn't an overseer anymore. Her friend put himself in charge of the group.

If Miriam hadn't done it first the other slaves would never have had the courage to come forward. It was too bad it had to happen that way; it would have been great to work with her friend. But it was too late now.

Miriam had no idea what her new overseer would be like. He was supposed to arrive in a few days though. She'd find out soon enough.

Part the Nineteenth

Dismounting from her dusty camel, Miriam walked around and stretched her legs. Leading her camel towards its stable, she saw a group of slaves gathered around a tall man.

"Is that the new overseer?" she asked the stableman.

"Yes," he answered. "He has brought some friends with him."

"I see," Miriam replied. So he had come. He had loyal friends; perhaps that was a good sign. But she wasn't going to take any chances. This had to be handled right.

Immediately she began to prepare. Miriam took extra care choosing her finest camel. She tacked him out with the best saddle, equipping it with all the accoutrements. They weren't going anywhere, but she tricked him out as if they were going on the longest drive possible. All the little details were accomplished with precision, exactly the way things were supposed to be for royal tastes and comfort.

Miriam herself was impeccably dressed in the costume of her profession. She took the camel's bridle and walked towards the overseer's pavilion, chin up. She led him right up to the overseer's chair and addressed him.

"Welcome to our group," she said. "I am Miriam the camel driver. I came to meet you and to let you become familiar with our practices."

"Thank you," he answered.

She proceeded to report, in brief but relevant detail, the requirements for the journeys. She pointed to each individual piece of equipment on the camel, describing their uses and the maintenance needed to keep them in shape. She described the outposts, the oases, and the correspondence between them all that was the only way to keep the royals happy and the drives successful.

"I am sure this is all familiar to you from previous experience, sir. I am sure you know how much work is required for these tasks to be completed, and I am very pleased to have your oversight in working with the other slaves to get things done."

"Oh, yes," he said. "I'm very familiar with camel drives. Wherever you go they are all the same. Thank you for showing me this. We should have no trouble working together."

Leading away the camel, Miriam felt satisfied with the way she had handled their meeting. He understood the work involved, and surely he would bring the other slaves in line.

She slept well that night.

Part the Twentieth

"I don't care to help you with the preparations."

The undisguised self-interest of this simple answer was a slap to Miriam. This slave had no right to speak to her this way. The camels needed the final preparations for the journey which was to start that day. Did this female think she could sustain her laziness indefinitely?

"We are all responsible to prepare the journey for the royals," Miriam said.

"Well, you should understand I am not going to be working very hard to assist you with the camel drives." She stood still with her arms folded and eyebrows lowered.

Miriam stared at this slave, speechless at her insolence. But the journey would not wait for them to sort it out. She turned on her heel, leaving the other slave behind. This only meant that much more work needed to be done.

In between double-checking all the details, she thought about what to do with this overconfident slave. “It was a good thing I already introduced myself to the new overseer,” she thought. “I’ll go to him, and he will bring this woman into line.”

Just as the journey was about to begin, a message came to her. It was from the head slave saying, “If you have to ask one of my people for something, you should ask me first. And if they say they are busy, they are.”

Miriam dispatched a message to the overseer immediately, requesting an audience upon her return. There seemed to be a lot of this ridiculous attitude going around. He would have to be the one to step in.

When the drive had finished and Miriam had safely returned, she hurried to get to the overseer's pavilion. This had to be nipped in the bud.

As Miriam approached, she saw that the head slave was already there. She seemed to be deep in conversation with the overseer: "…so you understand how much work you are talking about. I know you can see the situation we are in."

The overseer looked up and saw Miriam. "Please come in," he said, gesturing to her. "You have come at just the right time."

Miriam walked forward and sat down next to the head slave. The woman would not look her in the eye. "I wanted to talk with you, too," Miriam told the overseer.

Part the Twenty First

Miriam faced her new overseer and the head slave who had been resisting helping her. To have both of them together was more than she had hoped for. The overseer needed to give that slave an understanding of what her duties were.

"Sir," she began. "As we discussed earlier, the camel drives are becoming more and more frequent. You know the Prince had me placed under you in order to have the assistance of this group. At the present time I am having great difficulty getting that assistance."

The overseer and the other woman exchanged glances. "I have been learning about this," he said.

Miriam kept going: "I cannot do all these preparations and the camel drives alone. Will you make your slaves available to complete the preparations?"

The head slave was staring holes in Miriam.

"Well," the overseer said. "I've been talking with the group, and we really have a conflict here."

"We can't do any of the preparations," the other woman said. "We have too much to do. There is no way."

Taking a deep breath, Miriam replied, "It is the duty of us all to assist the royals. Your people are an important part of the success of these journeys."

"No," the overseer said. "They cannot help with this. That is your job, Miriam."

Miriam looked at him. She looked at the head slave. "But I see you finishing your work long before I'm done. And you start your work after I've been working for hours." Turning to the overseer, she asked: "How is it they can't help with the journeys?"

"I've gone over this," the woman interjected. "I don't want to talk about it anymore."

"Yes, you should not be involved in this," the overseer told the head slave.

"What do you want me to do? This is more than I can handle." Miriam struggled to keep her voice even.

"Just do your best," he said.

Part the Twenty Second

"I can't believe you came. It's been so long!" Miriam could not resist embracing her friend once more.

"I missed you," Hannah replied. "How long has it been since you moved away from our city?"

"Years," Miriam answered.

"It hasn't been the same without you." Hannah smiled at her.

"Well, the famine changed a lot of things." Miriam felt drunk with happiness to see her. It was amazing to remember how things used to be. Hannah had known her when things were very different in Miriam's life.

"So tell me all about everything!" Hannah said. The famine had hit her hard, but she still had her generous spirit. Miriam began to tell her everything that had been going on—all her troubles with the first overseer and how the royal friend came to help her.

"Well, what's happened since then? Did you finally get the help you needed?"

Miriam sighed, "No…" And the story of the other slaves came next.

"That's unbelievable. I cannot imagine how your new overseer allows it." She shook her head. "But Miriam, that's only your work. You don't really care about that. What about your lute?"

Miriam glanced at the dark corner where the lute had been relegated. "I do care about my work, though. You should see how fine the camels are now, especially when you compare to how they were when I first came." She told more and more about the things she'd done to elevate the camels to world-class quality.

But as she was talking, she couldn't resist going over to the corner to pick up the lute and tune it. It had been a long time since she'd played for Hannah. She had some new songs for her. They were from months ago, but they were new to her friend.

"Play for me," Hannah begged. And Miriam did. The music flowed out of her, and she stretched her talents like her legs after a long journey. She was stiff; it had been too long. But it felt so good.

When she was done, she looked at Hannah. Her friend was smiling as tears fell over her cheeks. Trying to speak, she took Miriam's hand. "Oh, Miriam. You cannot leave your lute behind like that again. You must stop being a slave."

Part the Twenty Third

"Stop being a slave? How could I do that?" Miriam looked at her friend, astonished. "Everyone has to work doing something."

Hannah flashed a sideways smile. "Miriam, I have learned a lot living through that famine. There are many ways to survive. Once you have faced your fears you become stronger. When you have been through the worst, you learn you can do anything."

"What are you saying?" Miriam looked at her friend. She could tell by the new lines in Hannah's face that she had been through hard times. But this tone in her voice was like a ray of sunlight.

"You have more choices than you realize. You think you are trapped, but the key is dangling from your own ring."

This kind of talk took Miriam's breath away. "But how? I have obligations. I am a slave here now. I can't just leave!"

Hannah shook her head. "Do you even know what you can and can't do? You have spent so much time worrying about the camels you don't even know yourself anymore, let alone what you can do." A big smile shined out from her face. "You've got what you need. You just have to find it."

Her heart started beating faster, just thinking about it. "I could maybe…If I…" and Hannah answered with more ideas. Perhaps there were things Miriam hadn't thought of.

"But, Hannah," Miriam said. "I like my camels. I have been able to make new paths and new routes that are making a real difference. I mean—I was not born a royal. I have to stick to what I know. It's not such a bad life."

Hannah looked at her. “You were not born a slave, either. You can have whatever life you choose to have. You can say your life is not so bad, but you are more than that, Miriam. You don’t have to settle for that kind of compromise. Your talent deserves more of you than the camels.”

Later that night, when they had gone to bed with sore throats from talking so much, Miriam stared at the roof with wide-open sleepless eyes. Hannah was her good friend and knew her better than almost anyone else. What she said seemed crazy, and there was no way to make it happen.

But making it happen was what Miriam wanted more than anything. Maybe…

Part the Twenty Fourth

"Come in."

Miriam stepped forward into the unfamiliar pavilion. She had come to him because he was the one in control of the money. Money is power. This man was very powerful, second only to the King.

Everything came down to money. That's what Miriam was discovering. As carefully as she could she had begun to ask around. What did it take to get out from being a slave? She didn't have to become a fugitive, did she? Surely there were legal ways to sever that bond.

Now it had come down to this. All the questions led to this place. The King's treasurer might be the only one who could say what her options were.

"Sir," she said, "I am Miriam the camel driver—a slave in His Majesty's service and also in yours." She bowed deeply. "I understand you are the one who keeps track of all the King's possessions, including his slaves. I am hopeful you will help me with some confusion I have."

"Miriam—yes, I know you." He smiled at her. "You have been doing an excellent job with the camels. We've been able to accomplish more with our long distance trade alliances lately than ever before. What can I help you with?"

Miriam kept her head down, still bowing low on her knees. This was the critical moment: her heart pounded as she replied. "I am most pleased to receive your appreciation, sir. I have worked hard to please the King and all the royal family. I have been a camel driver for many years, so it is very familiar to me. I must confess, however, it is a strange thing for me to act in the role of a slave. I have some questions about what it means to be the King's slave. Perhaps you can tell me more about that connection."

"Of course." He moved some record tablets on the table in front of him as if to arrange his thoughts. “You know we have many slaves here. The association can be created between the person and the royal family at any time that new projects or new work is identified. Of course we have a number of persons who are already acting as slaves. If our current slaves can do the work we do not take on new slaves.”

“Have slaves ever ceased to be slaves?”

He looked down with seriousness. “Yes, certainly. There are times when a slave does not perform the work they are there to do. They don’t fulfill the duties we expect—the duties that make them worth their upkeep. Those are the ones we choose to release and banish from our city.”

“I see. But do the slaves ever become free for good reasons?”

“Of course. Any royal person can buy the slave’s freedom by reimbursing the upkeep price—the price of 6 months upkeep. Even a friend or a member of a different family can buy a slave's freedom. All they need is the price."

Part the Twenty Fifth

The words of the King's treasurer circled in her head: "All you need is the price." Freedom was very much in her grasp. It was only a matter of counting the silver pieces—stacking them high enough. It was a known quantity now. Everyone knew how much it cost for upkeep.

Naturally that was only the first part. Freedom might seem wonderful for the first day. But the next day you had to have a place to live. You had to find your own food and clothing. That was a different stack of gold. A person needed a much bigger stack to take care of life's necessities all alone.

"To be honest," Miriam thought, "I have not had to think about how much gold I have. I knew that my needs would be taken care of by the royal family. I didn't have to think."

The camels still needed her. They took every minute she had to get them ready and to get the other things ready for the drives. "I've never had time to worry about accumulated things I don't need. I hear the other slaves haggling with their bill collectors and avoiding their gambling debts. I never was interested in those things. I haven't counted my money in a long time."

The present journey was a long one including many stops. Her friends and fellow slaves at all the stops were welcoming. And at the end the royal leader of the drive thanked her with a small bag of money, as was the custom. "I have gotten a lot of these little bags after all these camel drives," Miriam thought with an inward smile. "When I get home I will take the time to count them."

Thoughts of freedom were exciting but Miriam had other thoughts that were frightening and sad. As for the slaves in the royal city, she had no regrets at the thought of leaving them. But the diligent workers in the other stops and oases—they relied on her to get things ready for the royals. She loved working with them and would miss them very much.

Freedom felt like a forgotten responsibility. It was more than a little scary to think of not knowing for certain where her next meal would come from. Where would she live? She used to live that way, but that was long ago. She was older and wiser now—not the young foolish person she once was.

Even in the midst of her fear Miriam smiled at the memory. Being young and foolish was grand. No, she hadn't had the nice clothes, full meals and warm home that she had become accustomed to. But she had been so full of hope and promise. Laughter and joy came easily.

It was hard to laugh now.

Part the Twenty Sixth

The key to the chest was hanging on Miriam's belt. It had been a long time since she'd pulled open her treasure chest all the way. Once she tossed the little bags of money she'd received for her journeys into the chest she would forget about them.

The little bags of money were not really significant. Miriam thought of them as just a token. But taking them all out this time made her realize how many voyages she had traveled. It had been so much work. All those camels. All those preparations.

After these years, Miriam felt as if she knew the slaves at the other stops better than she knew her own neighbors. She had come to think of them as her team. They were the ones she could rely on. They had accomplished some amazing things together.

She piled up the bags, untying each opening and pouring out the gold and silver. It was exhilarating to think that she had accumulated this money. She had worked hard for all of it.

The voyages had been so much of her life, taking almost all her thoughts. She'd hardly had time to think about what it meant. Miriam had just concentrated on the next step needed to make the drives happen. The steps had taken her farther than she realized.

Probably that was what Hannah was trying to tell her. But Hannah didn't quite understand. The work she was doing had a lot of rewards, too. Sure, in this town she was a slave. But that was how it had to be. If there weren't any royals there would be no need for camel drives. Miriam by herself had no reason to make the trade negotiations; that was something for royals to do. But she loved to drive the camels. The royals needed her, but she needed them as well. They gave her the opportunity to lead the camels and to go on all the journeys.

It was good not to have to think about money. It was pleasant to trust that she would be provided for—that she would have everything she needed. And the work with the camels was not bad; she loved working with them and making the royals happy. Maybe there wasn't a problem. Everyone had to work, and everyone had things about work that they didn't like.

The money was piled around her. Miriam had counted it all, and now she knew. She had enough money to be free. More than enough. She would have some left over to take care of herself for quite awhile.

"I just don't know," Miriam thought. "This is a very big step. I don't think I could just strike out on my own. The world doesn't work like that. I'd better just stay where I am."

Miriam frowned. "It's not that bad."

Part the Twenty Seventh

Miriam was very proud of what she had accomplished. She knew without a doubt that she had every right to be. Her camels were healthy and strong. She had taken the scruffy, underfed camels and grown them into a herd nearly three times the size.

While the camel drives stretched on, she cherished these accomplishments. "They never did so many drives before I came. I know this overseer thinks it would have happened regardless of my presence, but I know better. I made this happen. I am changing this whole kingdom in my little way."

She passed the other slaves in the course of her day. The head slave and her friend sat and braided one another's hair as Miriam rummaged through their supplies to get what she needed. They had stopped speaking to her—quite satisfied with their own company and utterly contemptuous of Miriam.

She disdained their contempt: "They can have their stupid lives of chasing down the latest clothes and frittering away their money on dice. I am changing things for the better." She ripped the brush through her camels' coats and rushed to get the drives ready. She had every reason to take pride in what she did. She didn't need to act like a slave and shunt the work off on other people. She had her self-respect in spite of being a slave.

But the days were long and the journeys were longer. She fell asleep every night exhausted and woke before she had time to remember her dreams. "I work harder than a slave because I am not really a slave in my heart," she excused herself. "I am a person with my own goals and my own life."

Her life was entirely taken over by the camel drives.

A major drive for the King himself was planned, and it would take her far away. So far away that the other usual drives would have to be handled by someone else.

“I cannot be in two places at once,” she told her overseer. “You will need to have the head slave and the other slaves take care of them.”

“Of course,” he answered. “Aren’t they doing the drives already?”

What was he saying? After he had expressly told them they did not have to? “No, sir, they do not help.”

“Well, I’m sure they will have no problem while you are gone leading the King’s journey. Don’t worry.”

Part the Twenty Eighth

"Miriam, tell me what to do."

"What's the matter?" She looked into this young slave's face and knew it had happened. While she was out on the King's camel drive, another important royal needed camels for a journey. No one could be found to lead them.

Now this young man who knew nothing about camels was here meeting her at the oasis. He had the camels and the royals and no idea what to do next. Miriam thought, "This is why I always have to have everything ready in advance." Two camel drives now had to be prepared—her own and this hasty one. The second one took extra work. Miriam had to double-check everything because nothing had been done when it had first started out.

"Why are you here?" she asked the young man. "Where is the head slave, or the other slaves that I already spent time training?"

He shrugged and raised his hands in futility. “They needed someone, and I was there. I asked about the other two women, but they were nowhere to be found. The overseer sent me.”

Nowhere to be found? Hadn’t she warned the overseer that a journey might be necessary? And the only slaves who had done these before were nowhere? What did they think would happen if she hadn’t been there to make sure it all came together?

Miriam jerked the bags around, double-checking and repacking everything. More work for her. There was no end to what she had to take care of. The young man tried to help as best he could, but explaining what needed to be done took extra time.

She had to focus on instructing the young man to get the camels through the journey. And she had to keep her mouth shut and save her outrage for the overseer. All through the rest of her camel drive she thought of what she wanted to say to him.

She sent him a message at the next oasis at her first opportunity. She sent the message to him and to the vizier. This was the King's journey she was driving after all. She knew she didn't get his attention, but the King should.

She heard nothing from him until she got back. When she returned to the city she hurried to put the camels away. She wanted to speak with the overseer.

At last she found him. "Did you get my message?" Miriam asked.

"Yes," he said. "But I think the important thing is that the journey was successful." He patted her on the shoulder and left.

Part the Twenty Ninth

Miriam mounted her own camel—the only one that belonged to her. She packed her lute and some supplies and rode out of the city.

Her thoughts were flying so fast. She could not keep up. It was necessary to get away. She had to think and she wanted the sand and the sun and the wind to brush past her face.

When the camel's stride had established its rhythm, she could begin to order her thoughts. She was able to begin to think about what she was trying to do.

All the things she worked for—what did they matter, really? No one had asked her to work this hard. No one had said: "Work hard and you will be rewarded with success."

People had, in fact, warned her not to work hard. Slave and overseer alike had said: don't work hard. Don't do such a good job.

Yes, the royals appreciated her work—in an abstract way. But even the Prince had said he didn't expect excellence from slaves. Why should slaves expect it from themselves?

Miriam knew they thought of her as a slave. She was a slave. But she did not think of herself as a slave. She thought of herself as…really, she did not think of herself at all. She mostly thought about what needed to be done next.

Her laugh came so sharp it surprised the camel. "Ha! Maybe that's it exactly. Maybe that's the difference between me and the other slaves. They think of themselves first and the work next. If they think of the work at all..!" Memories of the other slaves' behavior, which had seemed incomprehensible before, suddenly made sense. If they had been thinking of their own pleasure first then their actions were perfectly logical.

"How absurd! What kind of system is this? The royals pay slave wages, give very little respect to their workers, and then complain about how their work is substandard. The overseers don't insist on quality—they themselves don't want to work hard. They don't want to be held accountable to a standard of quality."

Miriam sighed. She scratched her camel's ears. Then she laid her head down on his strong neck.

"There is no way to win."

Part the Thirtieth

Miriam had come to a small oasis with her camel and her lute. She stopped there to rest and think. As the camel drank its fill, she played her lute.

Her fingers moved over the strings. Music flowed over the sand singing out all her frustration, anger and confusion. She played. She played hard until she melted. Then Miriam played back into joy until the sand below and the stars above swelled with glory.

She stopped. Her face shone glorious too. "It can't be that bad!" Miriam told her camel. He kept chewing his cud.

"What can be wrong when I can make music? Slave, free—what does it matter? What difference is there really when I can make the world a beautiful place with my art?"

She got up and spun around arms flung out wide. “Nothing else matters!”

She saddled up and mounted the camel again. Her thoughts followed a new path this time. All she would need to do is speak plainly to the overseer. Just tell him straight out that she needed help, in words he would understand. He would listen. The royals needed her too badly; he would have to listen if she put it to him.

And once she had help she could work hard and still be able to play hard. That was the important thing.

First thing in the morning, Miriam washed her face and prepared herself. “This is the day,” she thought, taking extra care to look well for her conversation with the overseer.

Tall and confident she strode to his pavilion. As she had hoped, he was there alone.

"Sir, I must speak to you about a matter of utmost importance." She looked straight at him, with her head held high.

"Of course—in a moment," he answered her. "Just let me finish this."

"This time," Miriam thought, "it will have to be different. I've asked for help too many times. This will take something different than the other times."

He was finishing up. He looked at her. "What is it?"

Part the Thirty First

Miriam set her jaw and looked her overseer straight in the eye. She took a deep breath and said:

"Sir, I have been the camel driver for this royal family for more than two years. During that time the camel herd has increased to more than twice the number. The journeys I lead for the royal family have become even more frequent."

The overseer looked at her standing there. "Yes, I know this."

"I came here from another city and became a slave to drive your camels. I had never been a slave before. I am bringing this to your attention for a reason. I began my work as a slave, but things have changed. In order for me to remain here, these changes need to be reflected in my work."

The overseer looked surprised. Good. Miriam went on: "I will need to be made a head slave with all due honor. I have come to the conclusion that if you cannot offer me this position, I will buy my freedom and leave for another town."

The overseer looked down. "I am glad you have come to me." He sighed. "I am pleased with how you've been taking care of the camels. Perhaps I have not told you so as often as you deserved it because I do trust you."

"Thank you, sir. I appreciate that. I want to be clear, however. I will have to know your answer by the end of the week. If we do not come to an agreement, I will be moving on."

"This shouldn't be a problem. You'll hear by next week if not sooner."

"I will wait to hear from you." Miriam nodded goodbye and left the pavilion.

As soon as she was out of his sight her legs turned to jelly. "I hadn't realized how terrified I was in there," she thought. Now she could feel the rivulets trailing down her back.

But it had worked! He had said it shouldn't be a problem. At last—finally—she could do the job the way it needed to be done.

"Once I have that position, that title," Miriam thought, "I will finally get the cooperation from the other slaves. There are so many tasks that others could easily do for me. He *said* it wouldn't be a problem."

Miriam could barely sleep that night. Her mind was full of plans for her camels.

Part the Thirty Second

The King himself was planning a journey with all his family and closest advisors. Miriam had been given advance warning of his plan—for which she was grateful. The royalty had finally learned they were much more comfortable when they let Miriam prepare in advance.

The trip was one week away, and everything was going as planned. This time Miriam knew it was more important than ever to lead this drive flawlessly.

When she had gone to him the overseer had said there would be no problem meeting her demands for change. But Miriam knew better than to believe anything he said. It was possible he would come back tomorrow to give her everything she requested. But he might not.

And if he didn't, she had a plan in reserve. The overseer never had access to the King. He'd probably never seen His Majesty even once. The

Prince made appearances once in a while but the King did not.

Miriam had frequent access to the King. She had even met his Queen. If the overseer came back with an answer she didn't like, she would take the opportunity to talk to the King about it during the camel drive.

But she had hopes that her overseer would come back with an answer she could accept. The days passed slowly waiting to find out.

"Miriam." A messenger stood at the camel pen. "The overseer would like to see you tomorrow afternoon."

That was a day earlier than she expected. What could this mean? Early was probably good. But only tomorrow would tell. She slept fitfully.

....

"Come in," the overseer said. "Have a seat." He gestured to the pile of rugs. Miriam sat down keeping her back straight and holding all her dignity.

"I've been thinking about the last meeting we had." He was toying with the fringe on his rug. "I appreciate your honesty, and we very much would like to keep you as the camel driver. But we are not going to change anything you asked us to."

"Offering nothing?" Miriam was thinking. "You should bite your forked tongue. This only makes it easy."

"Thank you for letting me know. I will not remain here. I will put in my request for freedom. I'll be gone in two weeks then."

The overseer was rearranging some vases. "I hope you'll keep doing your job during that time."

Miriam smiled as she thought of the King's drive, now only two days away. "Don't worry. I will keep on doing my usual tasks until I leave."

Part the Thirty Third

What an insult! The overseer had offered her nothing to stay. “He has no respect for my work at all,” Miriam thought. “I always knew deep down they never appreciated me,” she thought. “I guess I hoped I was wrong.” It was painful to lose her illusions.

She was not wrong. No effort to retain her was exerted. She was put out like the trash. “The royals appreciate me,” Miriam thought. “How many times have I heard them say how much they appreciate what I do? Many of them have said I am the embodiment of what they are looking for in a servant.”

“No wonder the overseer wants me gone. He would feel very uncomfortable with the comparison of his service to what I provide. Well, he will get his just desserts,” Miriam thought. “I’ll keep right on doing what I do, and I will very much enjoy telling the King to his face that I am leaving. I would love to give the explanation when he asks 'Why?'"

She tried to make light of her dilemma, but the truth was heavy. Miriam felt sick. The hot angry tears left a big damp stain on her camels back. There was nothing left but self-respect. The overseer saw nothing but a slave when he saw her. "I am more than that! I am so much more! He does not deserve the good things I have to offer."

She couldn't even bear to touch her lute and face what she was feeling. Everything felt like a bruise. But morning followed night nevertheless.

She had dispatched messengers to the outposts to let them know she was leaving. She owed them that courtesy, for all the kindness they'd showed her on her travels. The next morning came back with messages—some well wishes and some outraged. 'How can you leave us?' they said.

This brought new tears. Oh, how hard it was. She wanted to keep working with the people who had been good to her. She wanted to turn the camel drives into the voyages of comfort, luxury and diplomacy she knew they could be. But the people in power would not let her. It was deeply wrong, and it stung like vinegar in a wound.

"I will send messengers to the Prince and others among the royalty," she said. "I know I will see the King next week, but I won't wait that long."

Part the Thirty Fourth

"You're to stay here. We have instructions to keep you from leaving this location."

Miriam had never expected this. The guards were at her door, and they were not leaving. Nothing had prepared her for this. She was imprisoned in her tent, and no one was telling her why.

She wanted to get out. She had to hear back from her messages to the oases. She knew the King was expecting her to lead the camels. But she was blocked with no reason given.

Not that she was without her suspicions. When she had sent those messages she had not expected anything more than questions from the people who received them. The overseer had never paid any notice to what she did before. But Miriam didn't think the overseer would have had the gumption to take such dramatic action.

It must have come from above. Whoever it was had taken notice of her honesty and put a stop to it. Miriam punched her pillow. “Isn’t that just like this city? No action taken but in the wrong direction. Why make things better when he—whoever he is—could use his power to protect the incompetence of others?”

She was trapped, but she couldn’t keep still. She paced across the floor. They weren’t giving her a chance! She only wanted to say a proper goodbye. It was true that she had hoped to have access to the King. She had hoped to tell her story that he might intervene on her behalf. But she wasn’t given that chance. All those people she had worked alongside—if they sent her a message now she couldn’t even receive it.

If only shc could gct a mcssagc out and explain what had happened. Didn’t they deserve to know? Maybe if she could get the attention of someone passing by she could get some help to send a message. She could find a private, safe way to communicate. She would circumvent the usual messengers and use her own. It's not like others hadn't done it.

She stopped. What would she say? She was done. There were no more tactics left. The last chance—speaking to the King—was gone. Nothing would happen. This was the end. She was done with her plans for the camels. There were no more journeys here.

It made her so angry. She had worked and worked to make these journeys smooth and comfortable, and this was her reward?

"I was right. There is no way to win." She wiped the tears from her face, punching her hands away. She dropped her hands to her sides and pulled them together into fists. "I knew this all along. The only way to win is to walk away."

But oh, it hurt to be treated this way!

Part the Thirty Fifth

Who had placed the guards at her door? How many people knew about her leaving? Miriam couldn't be sure that her messages had gotten through. She was stuck in her tent. No more time to plot, and nothing else could be discovered.

She desperately wanted to speak to the people who had been helping her—who relied on her. But the guards only allowed one destination: the city gates to buy her freedom and be on her way.

She gathered all the things that were her own while the guards watched. They made certain she took nothing that belonged to the King. They brought her camel to her, wearing only the worn saddle and bridle she rode in on. With her money, her trinkets and the few other things belonging to her packed up on the camel, the guards led her to the gate.

The treasurer's clerk was efficient. He did his job well. Miriam smiled at the irony. If only the slaves she had worked with had been like that she would never have had to leave. With her freedom papers signed, the guards left her, and she stood outside the gate holding her camel's leads.

Miriam stared back at the gate. She'd felt safe inside it—busy and important. She had handled her business with distinction and carried herself with respect. Now she was blocked out and had no idea what others knew or thought of her.

Did anyone other than her overseer even know she was gone?

Her eyes were full as she stared down the familiar and now-forbidden entrance. So many times she had led the camels through to fanfare. Now she was exiled. She stared unfeelingly for a long time before she recognized the figure approaching.

The vizier was at the gate on his stallion. He was making his rounds to be sure the royal city was safe and secure. Few people stopped him on his rounds; no one wanted to attract his attention and incur his purple-faced temper. Miriam felt a spasm of accustomed dread as he approached.

But she was free now. She had nothing to fear from him. But she did have one more thing she wanted from him.

"Your highness!" Miriam called out boldly.

Part the Thirty Sixth

"Good afternoon, Miriam." Smooth as butter, the vizier turned to answer her.

Miriam could not tell what he might know. Her ingrained timidity for royalty made her answer politely. "Good afternoon, sir." Her feelings throbbed in her throat.

"What can I do for you?" This was more politeness than she was used to receiving from this man. Surely, he was not unaware. This knowledge hardened Miriam's resolve.

"Sir, have you received my message?"

His eyes flickered. "Yes, I received it, and I was very disappointed to read it."

"Why?"

He looked down at her from his stallion. "The message reflected badly on areas that are my domain. I would much rather you had come to me with your problems." His eyes flicked to the document in Miriam's hands. "It seems it is too late now. That's a shame."

So he did know. His overly polite tone revealed his composure. Clearly he had instigated her exile. But did he really imagine that she would have been able to speak to him about her troubles? What kind of mirror did he see himself with? Did he have selective memory regarding his threats and rages when things did not go as he wished? He had always been a source of punishment—not help.

Miriam looked back unflinchingly. "Well, here we are."

He did not break her gaze. "Yes, we are."

There was one last thing Miriam needed to know. "Am I banished?"

The vizier pulled the stallions reins and wheeled around. "With regard to that, I respect the

King's wishes. Goodbye, Miriam. It was a pleasure working with you." He did not look back at her as he rode away.

Part the Thirty Seventh

Barred. Cast aside.

Miriam had been the one to leave. But at this end she felt much more like she'd been kicked out. At this point who would know? Who would tell the real story?

Her mind still raced with all the tasks left undone for the King's upcoming journey. She stared at the guarded city, aware of all the things that only she knew. She worried about it; she almost wished she could sneak in messages to let the slaves know what was needed to make it go off well.

But it wasn't her place anymore. They didn't even want her to help. They wanted her out of the city.

She turned her back. All the efforts and careful tending she had done had vanished. She spent these years of her life making a structure—a monument—that had come so near to completion.

Walking away, Miriam could still see it all in her mind—the details she had thought out and tested so thoroughly. She had created and established order. She had done all that—no one else.

"What will happen to the camels now?" she thought. She knew certain things that had not been done for them yet. Someone else had to take over. She should leave some instructions.

But no, that was done. Her work was finished. It had been handed over to the moths and rust.

Miriam let the bitter tears come. She turned over in her mind the brilliant pieces of her plans. She couldn't let those go so quickly. They shone as something worthy—something to attain. But they were not meant to be.

Her mind was wrestling to let go of these phantoms. Only her ingrained guiding instincts from the camel drives led her safely to shelter. Her camel stopped to drink before Miriam realized where she was.

She slid off to make camp. Her head was buzzing and her body was numb, but her camel needed respite.

"I suppose I should rest, too. This is very hard."

Part the Thirty Eighth

Miriam shook out her hands. Sitting next to the quiet oasis water, she had played her lute until her tender fingers throbbed and went past the pain. She played all the music she knew and then all the music her fingers made on their own. Her hands couldn't take anymore so she had to stop.

The soft breeze and the dusking blue of the evening sky made a bigger space than anything she had ever seen before. Unlike crawling from one spot to another during the camel drives, Miriam felt free to go—even fly—any direction at all.

She smiled to the sky. "To think! This was here the whole time. Whatever anyone said, I was never a slave except when I let myself be one. I am free to do what I want most—always."

Then she looked down. "Their tradition of slavery may be long-standing, but I was not meant to be a slave." She sighed, once again flooded with shame. How could she have let all this happen?

"I suppose I believed more in the vision of how I wanted things to be than I believed in what was really there. Nobody wanted my vision."

Miriam raised her head and set her jaw. "I still believe in my vision. True, it can't be for that city anymore, but I take it with me. I am going to find a place where my vision won't be wasted."

She reached for her lute again to play a song of her very own to the pool of water at her feet. She knew this water: it started as a river far away. It had travelled underground for a long way until it appeared here as a place of life and respite.

Her song lifted her and spread across the sky like blue. The vibration of the strings became the thrum of Miriam's heart. The song died away, and she remained. The stars were shining brightly in the inky sky.

"I don't know what happens next," she told her camel. "You have enough corn and barley in your feedbag, don't you? You're not worried about anything." She scratched his ears.

"I won't worry, either. Perhaps I will be wiser now."

www.ingramcontent.com/pod-product-compliance
Ingram Content Group UK Ltd.
Pitfield, Milton Keynes, MK11 3LW, UK
UKHW040601210726
13854UKWH00008B/1668

9 781411 654839